D0469335

WELCOME
PASSPORT TO READING
A beginning reader's ticket to a brand-new world!

Every book in this program is designed to build read-along and read-alone skills, level by level, through engaging and enriching stories. As the reader turns each page, he or she will become more confident with new vocabulary, sight words, and comprehension.

These PASSPORT TO READING levels will help you choose the perfect book for every reader.

READING TOGETHER
Read short words in simple sentence structures together to begin a reader's journey.

READING OUT LOUD
Encourage developing readers to sound out words in more complex stories with simple vocabulary.

READING INDEPENDENTLY
Newly independent readers gain confidence reading more complex sentences with higher word counts.

READY TO READ MORE
Readers prepare for chapter books with fewer illustrations and longer paragraphs.

This book features sight words from the educator-supported Dolch Sight Words List. This encourages the reader to recognize commonly used vocabulary words, increasing reading speed and fluency.

For more information, please visit passporttoreadingbooks.com.

Enjoy the journey!

Little, Brown and Company
Hachette Book Group
1290 Avenue of the Americas, New York, NY 10104
Visit us at lb-kids.com
mylittlepony.com

First Edition: April 2017

Little, Brown and Company is a division of Hachette Book Group, Inc.
The Little, Brown name and logo are trademarks of Hachette Book Group, Inc.
The publisher is not responsible for websites (or their content) that are
not owned by the publisher.

Library of Congress Control Number 2016956019

ISBNs: 978-0-316-43166-8 (pbk.); 978-0-316-55370-4 (ebook); 978-0-316-55369-8 (ebook);
978-0-316-43163-7 (ebook)

Printed in the United States of America

CW

10 9 8 7 6 5 4 3 2 1.

Passport to Reading titles are leveled by independent reviewers applying the standards developed by Irene Fountas and Gay Su Pinnell in *Matching Books to Readers: Using Leveled Books in Guided Reading*, Heinemann, 1999.

Licensed By:

My Little Pony

We Are Family

written by **Magnolia Belle**

LITTLE, BROWN AND COMPANY
New York Boston

Attention, My Little Pony fans!
Look for these words when you read this book.
Can you spot them all?

Castle of Friendship

magic

bakery

sports teams

In Ponyville, family is as important as friendship!

Twilight Sparkle is a part of many families.

Twilight lives in the Castle of Friendship
with Spike.
He is her best friend!

She also lives with her pet,
Owlowiscious.

Twilight loves Spike and Owlowiscious.
They are a family!

Twilight loves her parents, too.
She is great at magic because
her parents are Unicorns, too!

Twilight has a brother.
Shining Armor is married
to Princess Cadance.

They have a baby named Flurry Heart.
Twilight is Flurry Heart's aunt!

Flurry Heart is not the only baby
in Equestria.
Mr. and Mrs. Cake's twins are named
Pound Cake and Pumpkin Cake.

Fluttershy also has a brother.

His name is Zephyr Breeze.

Twilight and Fluttershy do not have sisters, but Pinkie Pie has three! They work with their parents.

Rarity also has a little sister.
She is very helpful.
Her name is Sweetie Belle.

Applejack has a brother and sister.

Big McIntosh and Apple Bloom

live with Granny Smith.

She takes good care of them.

Rainbow Dash does not have
a sister or brother.
She is an only child.
She looks out for Scootaloo
like a big sister.

Sometimes brothers and sisters fight
and hurt one another's feelings.
And sometimes they are the
best of friends.

Princess Celestia and Princess Luna
were mad at each other.
Now they are friends again.

Sometimes families live together
or get together for parties...

...like the Apple family.

And sometimes the ponies and friends who live together become a family, like Twilight and Spike.

Fluttershy has lots of pets.

She treats them like family.

They love Fluttershy very much.

Opalescence is Rarity's cat.

She is part of her family.

Pinkie lives with the Cake family.

She works with them in their bakery.

They help one another like family.

Sports teams are another
kind of family.
The Wonderbolts train
together every day.

Best friends are also like a family.

The Cutie Mark Crusaders are

like sisters.

Twilight, Applejack, Fluttershy, Rarity, Pinkie, Rainbow Dash, and Spike are close friends and make up a special family.

No matter where a pony lives,
they are with their family
when they feel love.